DATE DUE

SEP 0 8 2010	

Why the Sea is Salty

A tale from Korea

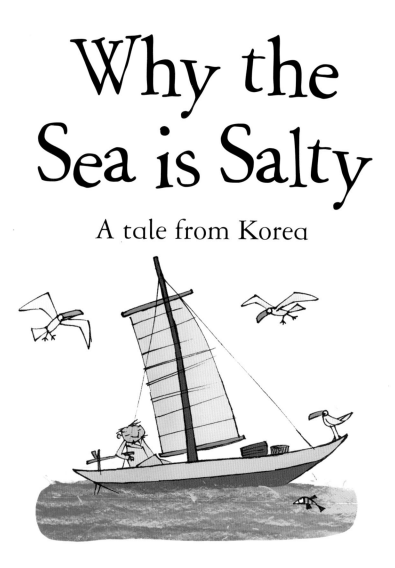

Retold by Rosie Dickins

Illustrated by Sara Rojo

Reading Consultant: Alison Kelly
Roehampton University

2

Long ago, the sea wasn't
salty like it is today. Once,
it tasted sweet.

3

So where did the salt come from? Well, it all began with a magic millstone...

This millstone belonged to
a great King.

5

Most millstones are used for making flour. But this millstone was different.

It made gold
and jewels...

or special spices...

or whatever the
King asked for.

The King's treasure chests
were always full. His food was
always delicious. And it was all
thanks to his magic millstone.

8

One day, a thief heard about the millstone. "I want it!" he thought.

"How can I find out where it's kept?" The thief scratched his head.

Then he put on his best
clothes and went to the palace.

11

The thief told the guards
he had come from far, far
away, just to see the palace.

12

A kind guard showed the
thief around. "These are the
gardens," said the guard.

No millstone
here.

"And that is the royal bedroom."

"I'm sorry not to see the magic millstone," said the thief. "I suppose it's hidden?"

16

"Of course," said the
guard, with a laugh. "It's the
King's greatest treasure."

17

"I bet I can guess where it is," said the thief. "Up a chimney?"

"No," said the guard.

"Under the floor?"

"No," said the guard.

"I bet you don't even know
where it is," teased the thief.

20

"Yes, I do," said the guard
proudly. "It's under the
King's bed!"

21

"What a clever hiding place," said the thief.

"And I suppose you have to
be a great magician to work
the millstone?"

23

"Oh no," said the guard.
"I've seen the King. You just
have to tap it like this..."

tap tap tap

"...and tell it what you want."

The thief left the palace, smiling.

Later, when no one was
looking, he crept back again.

He tiptoed into the King's
bedroom and reached under
the bed...

The thief hid the millstone under his cloak. And he ran away as fast as he could.

He ran all the way to the
sea. There, he leaped into a
boat and sailed away.

29

Out at sea, he looked at the millstone. "What shall I ask for first?" he wondered.

"Maybe some food would help me think."

He got out a bun and took a big bite. "Pah!" he spat. "That needs salt."

31

He grinned. "I know what to ask for..."

At once, the millstone
began to turn. Bright white
salt poured out.

The thief put some salt
on his bun and munched
away happily.

Then he fell asleep,
dreaming of riches.

All night long, the
millstone kept turning.

36

The pile of salt
grew bigger...

and bigger...

and BIGGER.

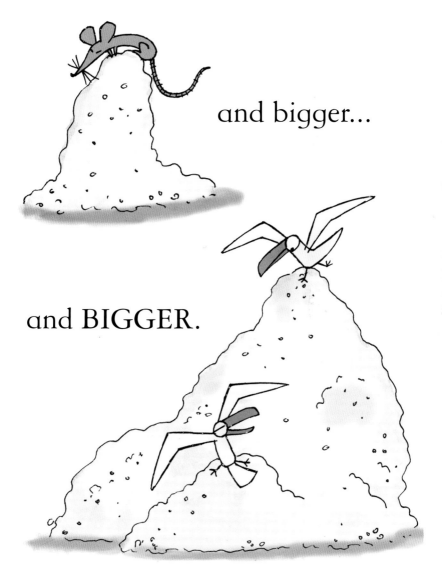

The thief was woken by
something tickling his feet.
"What's that?" he cried.

It was a HUGE heap of salt.

"Stop!" he shouted.
But the millstone kept turning.

"That's enough!" he yelled.
But the millstone kept turning.

41

The salt was very heavy.
The boat began to sink,
lower and lower.

Soon, waves were slopping over the side – and still the millstone kept turning.

The thief dug through the
salt, looking for the millstone.
But it was buried too deep.

The millstone kept turning...
The boat sank. It took the
magic millstone with it, right
to the bottom of the ocean.

There it has stayed, pouring out salt to this very day. And that's why the sea is salty.

46

As for the thief, he had to
swim home – where an angry
King was waiting for him.

Why the Sea is Salty
is a traditional folktale from Korea.
A similar story is told in Sweden.

Designed by Michelle Lawrence
Series designer: Russell Punter
Series editor: Lesley Sims

First published in 2009 by Usborne Publishing Ltd., Usborne House,
83-85 Saffron Hill, London EC1N 8RT, England. www.usborne.com
Copyright © 2009 Usborne Publishing Ltd.